"Scooter," Jake's voice sounded funny, as if she were afraid. "Do you see something in the hole?"

I looked carefully. Jake was right. There was something there.

"Let me get the flashlight so we can see what it is," I said. I raced to my room and back.

"Be careful," Jake said. "Maybe it's alive."

I shook my head. "No. If it were alive, it would crawl out."

"Maybe," Jake said. I don't think she was sure.

Carefully, not sure what I'd see, I shined the flashlight into the hole in Jake's room.

Be sure to read all of
The Adventures of Scooter and Jake

Cat Burglars?
Here Boy!

Gayle Roper

ChariotVICTOR
PUBLISHING
A DIVISION OF COOK COMMUNICATIONS

Chariot Books is an imprint of Chariot Victor Publishing,
a division of Cook Communications, Colorado Springs, Colorado 80918
Cook Communications, Paris, Ontario
Kingsway Communications, Eastbourne, England

CAT BURGLARS?
© 1995 by Gayle G. Roper for text and J. Steven Hunt for illustrations

Cover design by Joe Ragont
Cover illustration by J. Steven Hunt
First printing, 1995
Printed in The Untied States of America
99 98 97 96   5 4 3 2

To obey is better than sacrifice.
I Samuel 15:22

CHAPTER 1

"That's enough work for one night," said Dad. He put his saw down and closed his toolbox. "Don't step in that hole in the floor, kids."

The people who lived in our house before us had messed up the floor in my room, and Dad was fixing it.

"Come on, Scooter," Dad said to me. "Come on, Jake. Let's go play ball."

"Coming!" I grabbed my jacket and my baseball glove.

I jumped into the car and landed on top of my sister Jake and her bony knees. *Oomph!*

"Get off me, Scooter Grady!" she yelled.

"Get out from under me!" I yelled back. "This is my side of the car!"

I stared at Jake and she stared at me. Then she climbed over to her side.

"Thank you, Jake," I said politely.

She made a face at me.

Jake's real name is Jacqueline Anne. I always kid her that she goes by Jake because she can't learn how to spell Jacqueline.

Jake is one year older than I am. She's eight and in third grade; I'm seven and in second. Most of the time, Jake is a great sister. Most of the time.

Dad pitched to me first, and I swung as hard as I could. I missed.

"That's the way to hit the air!" Jake yelled.

I acted like I couldn't hear her. I knew I'd hit the next one out to her. Or the one after that.

And I did. I even hit one over her head. I cheered as she chased it.

"Okay," called Dad. "You kids switch places."

Jake and I were running past each other when I heard something. I stopped, and so did she.

"What's wrong?" she asked.

"Did you hear that?" I asked. I pointed to the tall grass at the edge of the field. "Listen."

She tilted her head. "I don't hear anything."

I walked to the tall grass and got real still. So did Jake.

"There it goes again," I said. "Did you hear it this time?"

Jake listened hard. "Yes," she said, excited. "I hear it! There's something in the grass!"

CHAPTER 2

Suddenly two tiny, tiny kittens came tumbling out of the tall grass. They stopped and looked at us for a minute, then ran right up to us and rubbed against our legs.

"Oh, Scooter!" Jake sat down and picked up the gray kitten. "Aren't they cute?"

I picked up the white one with a black patch over his eye. When I held him near my face, his little pink tongue darted out and he licked me.

Boy, what a rough tongue! We have a collie, but his tongue is soft. Not like the kitten's tongue!

"Dad, look!" I ran to him with the kitten in my hand. "Somebody must have dropped them off here because they know kids come to play ball. Can we take them home?"

Dad patted my kitten and didn't say anything.

I hugged Patch. I'd already named him because of the black mark over his eye. He looked like a furry little pirate.

Jake held her kitten in her arms, rocking her like a baby.

"Her name's Gruffy, because she's gray and fluffy," Jake said. "Oh, Dad! Don't you love her?"

You have to understand about our dad. He's a really nice man. He loves Jesus, and he loves Jake and me and our mom. But he doesn't love cats. Sometimes I think he doesn't like animals at all.

"All children need a pet, Marlin," my mom said to him when our dog was given to us. "The kids will learn to take care of him. And he'll love them and play with them."

Andy, our collie, does love us and play

with us, but Mom is the one who takes care of him. She feeds him and puts out his water and brushes him.

"We'll take care of the cats, Dad," Jake said. "We promise."

"Sure," Dad said. "Just the way you take care of Andy. Now put the kittens down, and let's play ball. That's what we came to do."

Jake took her turn batting, but it was hard for her. Gruffy sat on her feet the whole time, and Jake was afraid to move. She didn't want to hurt her.

She did hit a couple of balls out to me, and I chased them with Patch chasing me.

It was almost dark when we put the bat and gloves in the car. Jake and I stood with our cats in our hands.

"Please, Dad," I said.

"Please, Daddy," Jake said. She only says "Daddy" when she's really, really upset.

Dad stared at us, then let out a long breath. "Okay," he said. "You can keep them."

Mom took us shopping to buy some cat food and litter and a litter box.

"We have to train the kittens to use the litter box for their toilet," Mom said. "But cats train easily."

And they did.

Jake and Mom and I were very happy with our kittens, and Dad was okay. It was poor Andy, our collie, who had a hard time.

If Andy walked near Gruffy, Gruffy's hair stood on end, and she arched her back and hissed. Once I saw the kitten actually punch Andy on his long, long collie nose.

"Bad Gruffy," I said. "Don't you do that again."

Gruffy ignored me, and the next time Andy walked anywhere near her, *slap, swat, hiss!*

When Gruffy was nasty like that, Andy

would turn around and walk away, looking so sad.

"Come on, Andy! Don't walk away," I yelled. "Come back here. All you have to do is bark, and you'll scare the little thing. Then she won't bother you anymore."

But Andy was too gentle and nice even to bark.

Patch didn't hiss at Andy. He ran beside Andy when the dog walked around. He ran in and out and round and round Andy's legs. Patch thought Andy was playing a wonderful game every time he went anywhere.

"Stop that, Patch," I said. "Don't be such a bother to Andy!"

Patch ignored me, just as Gruffy did.

Sometimes, when Patch was running circles around his legs, Andy would just stop and stand still, because he was afraid he would step on Patch if he moved.

But there was one thing Patch loved even more than chasing Andy's legs. His favorite game was to jump up and bat his tiny paws at Andy's long, feathery tail. *Grab! Slap! Pull that hair!*

Andy could feel something pulling his tail, but when he turned to see what was wrong, he never saw anything. Patch always ran back between Andy's legs before he got caught.

"The kittens are so naughty," I said to Mom. "They don't listen to me at all."

Mom nodded. "Cats do what *they* want to do, not what *you* want them to. You want them to obey, but you can't get a cat to do that."

I felt sorry for Andy, getting picked on in his own house.

Then one day I found him lying in the sun. When he looked at me, he smiled. A collie's "ruff" is all the hair he has around his neck—and those two kittens were fast asleep in Andy's ruff. Patch's little nose was sticking out from one side, and Gruffy's little bottom was sticking out the other.

It's a good thing the cats became Andy's friends, because Andy turned out to be the one who saved their lives.

CHAPTER 4

I came home from school one day and called Patch.

Andy came, but Patch didn't.

"Where's Patch?" I said.

Andy didn't answer, but he bumped me with his nose. I petted him.

Jake came in the front door. "Here, Gruffy," she called.

Andy walked to her, but Gruffy didn't.

"Where's Gruffy?" she asked.

Andy didn't answer, but he bumped her with his nose. She petted him.

I went to my room and looked under the bed. No Patch.

Jake went to the living room and looked on the back of the sofa. No Gruffy.

I went to the kitchen and looked on the kitchen table. No Patch.

Jake went to her room and looked on her

pillow. No Gruffy.

"Where could they be hiding?" I said.

Andy came to me and bumped me with his nose.

"Not now, Andy," I said. I pushed him away.

He looked at me with big, sad eyes.

"Listen," said Jake. "Do you hear something?"

Very, very softly, I heard the kittens meowing.

"They're crying!" said Jake.

We ran all over the first floor, but we couldn't find the cats. Their meowing was loudest in the living room, but Patch and Gruffy weren't in the living room. We even took the cushions off the sofa and chairs in our search.

"Upstairs," I said. We searched the whole second floor.

The meowing was loudest in Jake's room, but the kittens weren't there. We even looked in the drawers of Jake's bureau.

Andy kept bumping me with his nose.

"Not now, Andy!" I said. "We have to find the kittens!"

I pushed him away.

We stood in the middle of Jake's bedroom and wondered what to do next.

Andy lay down in the middle of Jake's room and rested his nose on the floor. He began to whine and bark.

Suddenly the meowing got louder.

"They're talking to Andy," Jake said. "But where are they?"

I lay down beside Andy and put my ear to the floor.

"Jake," I yelled. "Patch and Gruffy are under the floor!"

CHAPTER 5

"Oh, Andy, you're wonderful!" I said. "You found the kittens!" I gave him a big hug.

He smiled and wagged his tail.

Jake lay down and talked to the kittens.

"Don't worry, Gruffy. It's okay, Patch. We'll get you out. You'll be all right."

She looked at me. "How did they get in the floor?"

"They must have crawled into the hole in the floor in my room," I said.

I ran to my room and lay down by the hole in my floor.

"Come here, Patch. Come here, Gruffy," I called in my nicest voice.

I tried to see inside the hole, but it was black. I ran to Mom and Dad's room and got Dad's flashlight. I shined it into the hole in my floor. I could see the pieces of wood that hold the floor up—joists, Dad calls them. In between the joists were open spaces just big enough for a pair of little kittens.

"Dad!" I flew downstairs when I heard him come home. "Dad! The kittens are caught in the floor!"

Dad wasn't very happy when he couldn't get the kittens to come back out of the hole in my room.

"Why won't they come when I call? Why won't they obey?" he said.

"Because you can't get a cat to do that," I said.

"They're caught, Daddy," Jake said. "We have to save them!"

Dad rolled up the rug in Jake's room. First he listened very closely to the cats to be sure where they were. Then he sawed a hole in Jake's floor.

I shined the flashlight into the hole, and there were our two little furry critters. They were lying on top of each other, and their eyes were big and scared.

Blinking at the flashlight, they hopped out of the hole. Jake grabbed Gruffy, and I grabbed Patch. They were safe!

CHAPTER 6

"I'm going to get a piece of wood to put over this hole and the hole in Scooter's room for now," Dad said. "Tomorrow's Saturday, and I'll make proper repairs then."

I nodded as I cuddled Patch.

"Now listen to me," Dad said, "both of you."

I nodded again.

"Look at me, Scooter. Look at me, Jake. Listen carefully."

When Dad spoke like that, he was very serious.

"I want both of you kids to forget about these holes," he said. "Don't play in them or near them. Just make believe they aren't there. And *don't* let those animals get in them again. Do you understand?"

"Yes," Jake and I said at the same time. "We understand."

21

Dad nodded and went down to the cellar to get some wood to cover the holes.

I went to my bedroom, carrying Patch. I put him down on the floor, and he climbed my bedspread like a hairy little mountain climber. He walked to my pillow, turned around several times, and lay down. He fell asleep right away.

I put my head on the pillow beside him and listened to him purr.

I meant to forget about the hole in my floor. I really did. But the more I tried to forget it, the more I remembered it.

Next thing I knew, I was lying on my stomach by the hole.

"Hey, Jake," I called. "Can you see this?"

I put my arm in the hole and shined the flashlight.

"Just a little," Jake called back. "But you'd better get away from that hole. 'Children, obey your parents' and all that stuff!"

I left the flashlight in the hole and went to Jake's room. Sure enough, I could see a little light coming from my room.

"Scooter." Jake's voice sounded funny, as

if she were afraid. "Do you see something in the hole?"

I looked carefully. Jake was right. There was something there.

"Let me get the flashlight so we can see what it is," I said. I raced to my room and back.

"Be careful," Jake said. "Maybe it's alive."

I shook my head. "No. If it were alive, it would crawl out."

"Maybe," Jake said. I don't think she was sure.

Carefully, not sure what I'd see, I shined the flashlight into the hole in Jake's room.

"Look!" I shouted.

"Is it alive?" Jake asked.

"Not at all," I said. "It looks like an old newspaper and a little box." I reached in to pull the things out.

Just then I heard Dad coming up the steps.

"You kids aren't near those holes, are you?" he called.

CHAPTER 7

Jake and I both dived onto her bed, and when Dad came into her room, we were sitting there as if we'd never done anything wrong in our entire lives.

Dad put the wood over the hole and rolled Jake's rug back into place.

"Stay away," he said. "I mean it!" He stood in the doorway and looked at us. Dad takes "Children, obey your parents" very seriously.

We nodded.

Dad went to my room and covered the hole. Soon he went downstairs to talk with Mom until dinner was ready.

I looked at Jake, and she looked at me.

"What are we going to do?" she asked.

"I don't know," I said. "But how can we just leave those things in the hole?"

"We have to get them," said Jake.

I nodded. "They might be important."

We tiptoed to the edge of Jake's rug and began to roll it up. Somehow the rug rolled better for Dad than it did for us. Jake ended up on her hands and knees, holding the rug off the floor with her back. I slid on my stomach to the piece of wood. I took it off the hole as quietly as I could.

"What if Dad comes up?" Jake whispered.

"We're in big trouble," I said.

"Well, hurry up!" Jake was nervous.

I reached in for the newspaper and little box. I pulled them out and crawled out from under the rug tent and put them on the bed. Then I crawled back under the rug and put the wood over the hole. Jake and I backed out, and the rug flopped back into place all by itself.

"Hey, kids!"

It was Dad, calling from downstairs. We must not have been as quiet as we thought.

We rushed to the bed and sat down, all innocent.

"You're not playing near that hole, are you?" Dad called.

"N-n-no, Dad," I said. "You told us not to."

"Okay," he said. "Good for you."

"You lied," whispered Jake. Her eyes were wide open.

"Well, when we answered, we *were* sitting on the bed, not playing in the hole," I said. "And what else could I say?"

"I don't know. I guess we'd better see what we found."

I spread the newspaper carefully and found several separate pages.

"Look!" Jake pointed to a picture in the middle of one page. "It's Allen Gibney from down the street! Only he looks younger than he is now."

I looked at the date at the top of the page. "This newspaper is old." I did some subtracting in my head. "It's nine years old!"

Jake nodded. "It says here that Allen Gibney was seventeen in this picture. That means he's twenty-six now. Old."

"Move your hand, Jake," I said. "I want to see what it says under the picture."

Jake read out loud, "Allen Gibney being taken to jail for the theft of the Muldoon necklace."

"What?" I couldn't believe my ears. "Allen Gibney went to jail?"

Allen Gibney lived with his mother and father, even though he was grown up. He worked at the hardware store that his father owned.

Mr. and Mrs. Gibney were nice, but Allen Gibney was always cranky, and I didn't like him much. Maybe jail made him cranky.

Jake pointed at the newspaper. "It says he stole a necklace that was worth lots and lots of money. It was made of diamonds and rubies. He said he didn't take it. And the police never found it."

Suddenly I looked at the little box. I opened the lid carefully, and we both gasped.

Diamonds gleamed and rubies glowed right there in my hand. We had the Muldoon necklace, and it was beautiful!

CHAPTER 8

Jake spread the other pieces of newspaper on her bed. They were all about Allen Gibney.

"Look," Jake said. "This picture was taken the day his trial began."

The picture showed Allen looking very angry, walking with a man who was his lawyer. Mr. and Mrs. Gibney were behind Allen. Mrs. Gibney had a tissue to her eyes.

"Poor Mrs. Gibney," I said. "She's crying."

Jake nodded. "Moms are like that."

We pushed the picture aside and looked at the last piece of newspaper. It had a big headline: "ALLEN GIBNEY FOUND NOT GUILTY!"

The picture showed Allen Gibney smiling, but somehow he still looked angry.

"Hey, kids!" Mom called suddenly.

Jake and I both jumped.

"Yes?" Jake called. She sounded guilty to me, but Mom didn't hear anything funny in her voice.

"Dinner's on the table. Come right away."

"Okay," I called.

"What do we do with this stuff?" Jake whispered. "We can't let Mom and Dad see it, or they'll know we were in the hole."

"Stick these under your mattress," I said. I pushed most of the newspapers into her hand. "I'll hide the rest in my room."

I ran to my room and pushed the necklace, still in its box, under my mattress. I also had the "not guilty" newspaper article, and I pushed it after the box.

Then I stepped back and looked at my bed. It was sort of lumpy because I don't make it very well, but no one would ever know it was the hiding place for a real treasure.

That night before I went to bed, I read the "not guilty" article. It took me a while, and I never did figure out all the big words, but I understood enough.

Allen Gibney used to work at the Muldoon mansion, cutting grass and doing things in the garden. Once he went inside the house for a glass of water. He said he never went anywhere in the mansion but the kitchen.

And he said he certainly never took any necklace!

The police felt he could be guilty, because he'd already done lots of little wrong things like stealing hubcaps and "borrowing" cars from his father's friends.

"I took cars without asking and went for rides," Allen Gibney said. "But I always returned them. I would never steal anything!"

Well, I wondered, if Allen Gibney didn't take the necklace, who did?

And how did the necklace get from the Muldoon mansion to Jake's bedroom?

And why was it still in our floor after nine years?

I lay in bed and thought for a long time. When I fell asleep, I had a plan to find out the answers to my questions.

CHAPTER 9

"Come on, Jake," I said quietly as soon as we had finished breakfast the next morning.

"Where are we going?" she asked.

I put my finger to my lips. "Shh!"

I tiptoed out the back door. She followed.

"Where are we going?" she repeated, this time in a whisper.

"To the Gibneys' house," I said.

Jake looked at me as if I were crazy.

"We can't go there!" she said.

"Sure we can," I said. "They all work at the hardware store on Saturday. I've seen them when I've gone shopping with Dad."

I started down the street, looking carefully to see that no one was watching us. Jake followed me.

"What are we going to do when we get there?" she asked.

"Search the house," I said.

31

"Scooter!" Jake was shocked. "We can't do that! It's wrong!"

"How else are we going to find out how the necklace got into our house?" I asked.

"I don't know, Scooter," she said as we crossed the street. We ducked behind the hedge in the Gibneys' front yard. "But we can't go into somebody's house!"

"We have to do this," I said. "We'll look for a diary or some clue or something. Then we'll know what happened."

Jake was unhappy. "Mom and Dad will be very angry if they find out."

"How are they going to find out?" I asked. "We're not going to tell."

"Are things wrong only if you get caught?" Jake asked.

But she followed me to the Gibneys' back door. I tried the doorknob. It was locked.

"Rats!" I said. "You'd think there were robbers in the neighborhood or something."

"Are we robbers?" Jake asked.

"No!" I said. "We're detectives."

We tried the basement door and the front door, but they were locked too.

I was about to give up when Jake

grabbed my arm.

"Look!" she said, all excited. "An open window!"

The window was halfway along the house, and it must have been left open for the spring breezes. There was no screen.

The problem was that neither of us could quite

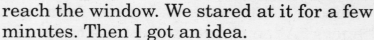

reach the window. We stared at it for a few minutes. Then I got an idea.

"I'll get on my hands and knees," I said, "and you stand on my back. Then you can climb in and open the back door for me."

I got down on my hands and knees, and Jake stepped on my back. I couldn't believe how heavy she was!

"Hurry up," I puffed. "You're killing me!"

Jake had one leg over the windowsill when a loud voice yelled, "Just what do you think you're doing?"

CHAPTER
10

It was Allen Gibney!

I jumped up and ran.

"Come on, Jake!" I yelled. "Let's get out of here!"

I was all the way across the street before I realized that Jake wasn't with me.

"Jake!" I called. "Where are you?"

I heard a little scream. It came from the Gibneys'! Allen Gibney must have caught Jake!

I ran back to the Gibneys' yard and hid behind their hedge. I peeked around it and saw Allen Gibney leaning out the dining room window. He had Jake in his hands and was pulling her into the house. Jake kicked and tried to get away, but she couldn't. Allen was too strong.

I had to save her! But how?

I sat on the ground by the hedge and

thought. I stared at a blue car parked at the curb and wondered how a kid could beat a grown-up man.

Suddenly it hit me. That blue car hadn't been at the curb when we first came. I was sure of that. What if it was Allen's car? Maybe the front door was unlocked now!

I tiptoed up onto the porch and tried the doorknob. It turned in my hand, and the door opened.

I stepped inside and shut the door as quietly as I could. I looked around. I was in the living room. I could hear a loud, angry voice from the back of the house. And I could hear Jake crying!

I tiptoed through the house until I came to the kitchen door. I peeked in.

Jake was sitting on a kitchen chair

sagging like a stuffed animal. She was crying and crying.

Allen Gibney was talking on the phone.

"We can't have things like this happening," he said.

He stopped and listened a minute.

"I know they're just kids," he said. He turned and stared at Jake. She cried harder.

"We didn't mean anything," she sobbed. "We didn't."

He paid no attention to her.

"I don't care what you say," he said into the telephone. "I think they need to be taught a lesson!"

CHAPTER 11

I looked at Allen Gibney's face. He looked
so mean!

Boy, was I scared. So was Jake.

Allen hung up the phone and walked
toward the refrigerator.

"You know something, kid?" he said to
Jake. "My best friend, Bruce, used to live in
your house. We used to do lots of stuff
together until he was killed in an
automobile accident."

Allen pulled the refrigerator door open.

"Everybody thought I was a really bad
kid and Bruce was a really good kid," he
went on. "But Bruce was worse than I ever
thought of being. I was just unlucky enough
to get caught all the time. Boy, did I ever get
caught. And for something I didn't even do."

Allen bent down and reached inside the
refrigerator.

While he was bent over behind the door, I waved at Jake, trying to get her attention. She was too busy crying to see me.

I saw that the door on the kitchen closet was partly open. While Allen was still buried in his refrigerator, I raced to the kitchen closet and jumped in. I pulled the door almost closed behind me. I left a little crack so I could see and hear.

Now I was closer to Jake, but she still didn't know I was there.

"Hey, kid," Allen said to Jake. "Do you want some iced tea?"

Jake looked at him with puffy eyes. "Me?"

"Who else?" Allen said. "Do you want some tea?"

Jake shook her head. "No, thank you."

Allen looked at her. "You have nice manners for a burglar," he said.

"I'm not a burglar!" Jake said. "I'm a detective!"

Allen looked at her in surprise. Then he started to laugh.

"A detective?" he said. "And just what are you detecting?"

"The Muldoon necklace," Jake said.

38

Allen stopped laughing. "What do you know about the Muldoon necklace?" he asked. He looked very mean now. He scared Jake so badly that she couldn't say a word.

Allen poured himself a drink. Then he turned and leaned into the refrigerator again, putting away the tea. While he couldn't see us, I ran out of the closet. I grabbed Jake's hand.

"Run!" I yelled.

I pulled her out of her chair, and we raced toward the front door and freedom.

"Hey, you two!" Allen called. "Come back here!" He started after us.

I pulled the front door open. Jake was right on my heels.

We ran right into the arms of another adult, who grabbed us and held us tight.

We weren't going anywhere.

CHAPTER 12

My face was pushed into the stomach of the person holding me, and I couldn't see anything. One of my arms was free, and I started hitting. Both my feet were free, so I started kicking, too. I had to get away! I had to get help!

"Stop that, Scooter! Stop that kicking this instant!"

When I heard that voice, I froze. Now I was really and truly in deep, deep trouble.

The man who had captured us at the door was our dad.

"So, you've got them, Mr. Grady," said Allen. "Bring them in here and we'll talk."

Our dad lifted us off our feet and carried us into Allen's house. He sat us down in the Gibneys' kitchen. He bent over and rubbed his leg where I had kicked him.

Then he stood up and looked down at us.

Boy, was he tall! And boy, was he mad!

"Just what do you two think you were doing?" he roared. "And your answer had better be good!"

"I'm sorry!" Jake said. She was crying again. "I'm sorry! We didn't mean to be burglars. Scooter said we were detectives."

Dad stared at her. "Detectives?"

Jake nodded her head. "Detectives."

"Scooter," said Dad. "You've got some big explaining to do."

I was glad I was sitting, because my knees were shaking like Jell-O. It was all I could do not to start crying as hard as Jake. "Please don't be mad at us," I said. "We were just trying to help. Honest, Dad. Honest."

CHAPTER 13

Dad looked at me as if I were crazy.

"How in the world were you going to help anyone by breaking into the Gibneys' house?"

"We were looking for clues about the Muldoon necklace," I said.

"And how do you know about the Muldoon necklace?" Dad asked.

"The newspapers said Allen didn't take it," I said. "We were going to look for clues to prove he didn't."

"That's why you were trying to climb in our window?" Allen asked.

I nodded.

"Scooter," said Allen. "Don't you think that if I had clues about the necklace, I would have given them to the police myself? I know people still think I stole it. I know I didn't, and so does whoever took it. But everyone else wonders."

"But the newspapers said you were found not guilty," I said.

"That means they couldn't prove I stole anything. But, believe me, people still wonder. I see the funny way they look at me at my dad's store."

Dad looked at me. "What newspapers are you talking about?" he asked.

"The ones we found in the—" I stopped and looked at Jake.

"We have to tell," she said. "Even if we get in more trouble."

I nodded. Jake was right. And I could see that obeying your parents could save a lot of trouble in the long run.

"The newspapers we found in the hole in Jake's room."

"We found the Muldoon necklace there too," Jake said.

"What?" Allen Gibney looked as if someone had punched him in the stomach. "You found the necklace?"

We nodded.

"Diamonds and rubies?" he asked.

"Diamonds and rubies," we said.

"It's at your house now?" Allen asked.

"Under my mattress," I said.

"Why didn't you tell me what you found?" asked Dad.

"You told us to stay away from the holes," I said. "We were afraid you'd be mad."

"Maybe a little mad, but not as mad as I am about you climbing into somebody's house."

Suddenly Allen rushed at us, scaring me half to death. He grabbed Jake and me.

"Oh, thank you! Thank you!" he said as he gave us a great big bear hug. "I can finally prove I didn't do it!"

CHAPTER 14

The police came to our house and took charge of the Muldoon necklace.

They talked to Jake and me about how we had found it. We showed them the holes in the floor. And we showed them Patch and Gruffy.

"The next time you find anything important," they said, "you call us, okay?"

They talked to Allen Gibney for a long time. They asked him lots of questions about his friend Bruce who used to live in our house.

Finally the police left.

Allen sat in our living room and shook his head.

"I can't believe Bruce stole the necklace," said Allen. "I thought he was my friend."

"I don't think he took the necklace to get you in trouble," said Dad. "I imagine he wanted to make some money selling it. He was probably very surprised when you were arrested."

"But he never helped me out." Allen looked very sad. "He knew I wasn't guilty, but he never said so. Would he have let me go to jail for something he did?"

"Who knows?" said Dad. "When you were found not guilty, he didn't have to decide."

"I think he must have been scared, Allen," I said. "He put the necklace in the floor to hide it. He put it in the hole in my room to keep it safe and pushed it under the floor until it reached Jake's room. Then he was too afraid to do anything else with it."

"And then he got killed," said Jake. "And nobody knew the necklace was here."

We were all quiet for a minute, thinking about Bruce stealing the necklace and poor Allen getting blamed for it.

Patch and Gruffy ran into the room. They saw Allen and walked all around his feet to check him out.

"Go away, cats," said Dad. "Leave Allen alone."

Gruffy lay down on one of Allen's feet,

and Patch climbed up the side of the chair and sat on Allen's lap.

"Why don't those cats ever listen to me?" Dad asked.

"You can't get a cat to do that," I said. "They only do what they want."

Dad nodded. "Like some kids I know," he said.

"You know why everybody believed I took the necklace?" Allen said. "Because I was always disobeying. Be careful, kids. Pay attention to your parents. Don't be dumb like me."

The doorbell rang, and I ran to answer.

"Are you Scooter Grady?" the man asked. "The boy who found the Muldoon necklace?"

I nodded.

"I'm from the *Daily Record,* and I'd like to take a picture of you and your sister."

"Come on in," I said. "You can put Allen

47

in the picture, too. And Patch and Gruffy. If they hadn't crawled into the floor, we wouldn't have found the necklace."

"Your cats?" said the man. "Will they sit still for the picture?"

I nodded. "If we pet them, they'll sit still. We can get our cats to do that."